The Boxcar Children Mysteries

THE MYSTERY ON STAGE

created by
GERTRUDE CHANDLER WARNER

Illustrated by Charles Tang

Albert Whitman & Company
Chicago, Illinois

Contents

CHAPTER 1

Stagestruck

One fall day, Jessie Alden stood outside a bookstore in Greenfield. In the window was a large poster:

WANTED

Actors, actresses to perform in
The Wizard of Oz

Auditions held Saturday, November 4th
9AM–4PM
Greenfield Community Playhouse
Scripts available in bookstore.

The bookstore was closed, but Jessie stood staring at the poster for a time. She did not even notice when another girl also stopped to look in the window.

"Oh, I love *The Wizard of Oz*," the new girl whispered aloud.

Jessie jumped and whirled around to face the girl. "I didn't think anyone else was here — you scared me," twelve-year-old Jessie said.

"I'm sorry, I didn't mean to," the girl answered.

Jessie smiled. "I'm Jessie Alden," she said. "Will you be trying out for a part in this play?"

The older girl did not return Jessie's smile. She seemed to look beyond Jessie, far off into space. "I'm Sarah Bellamy," she finally answered. "And yes, I will be. I want the part of Dorothy." Sarah spoke in a deep, clear voice.

"Oh, I'd like to try for that part, too," Jessie said. "I've never tried out for a big role like that before. Have you?"

"Why are you asking me that?" Sarah asked sharply.

"I'm sorry," Jessie said, looking down at the sidewalk.

Sarah looked a little ashamed of herself. "I didn't mean to snap at you," she said as she pulled her purple coat more tightly around her shoulders. "I'm just in such a hurry. You must excuse me."

Before Jessie could say another word, Sarah turned and walked quickly away. Jessie stared after her. Sarah's long dark hair blew in the wind. Her hair and her purple coat seemed to float around her body as she moved down the street. "She looks just like a dancer," Jessie said aloud.

Suddenly, a big gust of wind blew a pile of yellow leaves from the trees. Jessie shivered and buttoned her red jacket before she, too, hurried home.

"Violet, you'll never guess what I saw!" Jessie exclaimed to her ten-year-old sister when she burst into her house.

Jessie was so excited, she let the front door bang behind her, which was unusual. Jessie never banged doors.

Violet looked up from the picture she was drawing of Watch, the family dog. "What?" she asked as she stretched her legs.

"Well, the Community Playhouse is putting on *The Wizard of Oz*." Jessie sank into her grandfather's overstuffed armchair. "I really want to try out for the part of Dorothy."

Watch ran to Jessie wagging his tail. "Oh, Watch," Jessie said, laughing. She patted Watch's soft fur. "I didn't mean to interrupt your portrait."

"He wasn't sitting still anyway." Violet shook her head and pretended to give Watch a cross look.

The front door opened again, and in came the girls' grandfather with their elder brother, Henry. Watch bounded over to Henry.

"Oh, Watch, can't you see my hands are full?" Henry, who was fourteen, laughed and nudged Watch with his foot. Henry and Grandfather were each carrying several logs of wood.

"Oh, good, you're building a fire," Jessie

said. "It will be cozy on a night like this."

"It sure will." Benny came into the living room from the kitchen. He held a half-eaten chocolate-chip cookie in his hand.

"These cookies just came out of the oven," Benny said proudly. "I helped Mrs. Mc-Gregor make them." Mrs McGregor was the Alden's housekeeper.

"Oh, Benny, don't spoil your appetite before dinner." Jessie tried to sound stern, but she couldn't help smiling at her six-year-old brother. He always seemed to be eating.

"Nothing could spoil Benny's appetite," Henry said. He crouched by the fireplace and lit the logs with a match. Soon a small fire blazed merrily.

The four Alden children looked happily around their big cozy living room, while the firelight flickered on the walls. They hadn't always lived with their Grandfather. In fact, after their parents died, they did not even want to meet him because they'd heard he was a mean man. They laugh about that now because nothing could be further from the truth.

When Grandfather found his grandchildren, they had been living by themselves in an old abandoned boxcar in the woods. It was a happy day for the family when he brought them all to live with him in his big wonderful house in Greenfield. He even moved the boxcar to his backyard, so his grandchildren could play in it whenever they wanted.

"Jessie has some exciting news," Violet announced to her family. "She's trying out for a big part in *The Wizard of Oz*."

"Oh, Jessie, that's wonderful." Grandfather came over to put his arm around his granddaughter. "I read about the play in the paper."

"I have some exciting news, too," Benny said. He wiped cookie crumbs onto his blue pants. "Soo Lee is coming to dinner with Joe and Alice."

Jessie beamed. "Oh, good! We haven't seen them in a long time."

Benny nodded. "I wonder if Soo Lee knows the story of *The Wizard of Oz*?"

"If she doesn't, I'm sure she'd like to hear it, Benny." Grandfather chuckled. He knew

Benny had a special fondness for his seven-year-old cousin.

"Alice told me Soo Lee is reading everything she can in English, and she's asking lots of questions," Jessie said.

Benny grinned. He remembered how shy Soo Lee had been when he first met her at the airport not too long ago. The children's cousins, Joe and Alice, had adopted Soo Lee from Korea.

When the doorbell rang, Benny was the first to answer. Joe swept him up in a big bear hug. Alice kissed each of her cousins in turn. Benny took Soo Lee by the hand and led her into the dining room.

At dinner, the Aldens ate roast chicken, mashed potatoes, peas, and salad. No one could stop talking about the play. "I could help you learn your lines, Jessie," Mrs. McGregor said as she put a bowl of cranberry sauce by Joe's elbow.

Jessie gave Mrs. McGregor a grateful look. "That would be wonderful," she told her. "I'm planning to go pick up the script tomorrow. The auditions will be held in two days."

"The what?" Benny asked.

"That's when you go and try out for the part you want," Henry explained to Benny.

Jessie nodded. "I really need to practice," she said. "I met someone today who wants the same part I do." Jessie told her family about the girl who rushed away as soon as Jessie started asking her about the play. "The strange thing is Sarah did not seem to be in a hurry until I started talking to her." Jessie finished her story and took a drink of water.

"It sounds like she didn't want you to ask her any questions," Henry pointed out.

"But why not?" Jessie asked.

"Jessie, not to change the subject," Grandfather said, "but maybe you should tell Soo Lee a little about Dorothy."

Jessie nodded. "Dorothy," she began, "is a little girl from Kansas who gets swept away to the land of Oz in a tornado."

"Her dog, Toto, goes with her," Benny chimed in.

Soo Lee nodded. "I know that story, Jessie. I saw the movie." Soo Lee looked at Jessie with her big brown eyes. "I think you'll be a very good Dorothy."

Alice laughed. "Soo Lee loved the part where Dorothy meets the Cowardly Lion and the Tinman."

"But I didn't like the Wicked Witch of the West at all." Soo Lee shook her head. "I'm glad you don't want that part."

Benny pushed his peas to one side of his plate. He seemed deep in thought. "Jessie," he finally said, "do you think Watch could try out for the part of Toto?"

Everyone laughed. "I don't see why not," Joe finally answered. He stopped laughing and wiped his eyes with his napkin. "Watch is well trained, and he would have no trouble following Jessie around."

"If Watch can get a part, maybe the rest of us should, too," Henry said. "I don't think I want to act, but I could build scenery or help with the lighting."

"And I could make costumes." Violet's eyes glowed. She loved to sew.

"Could I do something?" Soo Lee looked at Jessie. "I'd like to."

"You could help paint the scenery, Soo Lee," Jessie said returning Soo Lee's smile.

Benny swallowed his peas with some effort. "I could train Watch for his part," he volunteered.

"Benny, there's a lot you could do," Henry said. "They probably need several people to help with scenery in a play like that."

"Well, it's all settled then," Violet said. "When you go for your audition, Jessie, we're all coming with you."

CHAPTER 2

Auditions

The day of the auditions was clear and cold. Jessie woke up feeling so nervous she could barely fasten the buttons on her polka-dot blouse. Violet came to her rescue.

"Jessie, it's not like you to be so jumpy. You're going to be fine," Violet assured her sister.

Jessie sighed. "I hope so. I think I'll feel better once we're there."

Alice dropped Soo Lee off at the Aldens'

just as they were finishing their breakfast. "Good luck, Jessie," she called. "I wish I could come to the auditions, too, but I told Joe I'd help him paint the porch steps."

As they were ready to leave, Mrs. Mc-Gregor came out of the kitchen to give Jessie a hug. "I'll be rooting for you," she said. Watch barked and thumped his tail on the floor. "And, as you can see, so will Watch."

Jessie managed a smile.

"Break a leg, Jessie," Grandfather called from his armchair as the children headed out the door.

"Grandfather, what do you mean?" Benny gave his grandfather a puzzled look.

"Don't worry, Benny. 'Break a leg' is just another way of saying good luck. Actors often use that expression." Grandfather waved good-bye.

The Community Playhouse theater was a fifteen-minute walk from the house. Soon the children could see the fancy brick building in the distance. A large park encircled the building.

The children crossed the lawn in front of

the theater. They passed big flower beds filled with orange and yellow chrysanthemums, now a little faded from the cold. Stone benches were placed underneath tall oak trees.

"It's pretty here," Soo Lee said, looking all around her.

Soo Lee had never seen the community park and theater before. She lived with Joe and Alice in a town not far from Greenfield.

"Well, we're here." Violet gazed up at the large building. Henry opened the heavy oak door, and the children entered a big lobby. People clutching scripts milled around the room.

A woman was seated behind a long table. She had several long sheets of paper on the table in front of her. "Please sign here for the part you're trying out for," she told the children. "The auditions will begin in half an hour in room 222 upstairs."

"Hey, look," Benny nudged Violet. "Why is that man in a costume already?"

Indeed, a man with a tin helmet covering his head headed up the stairs. He wore a metal barrel around his body and silver tights on his legs and arms.

"I don't know," Violet answered. "But that's a wonderful costume for the Tinman. Maybe he feels it will bring him luck."

Jessie passed the sign-up sheets to Henry who wrote his name under scenery and lighting. Violet signed up to help with costumes.

Soo Lee added her name under scenery and passed the sheet to Benny. Benny was so busy looking at the Tinman's costume, he didn't pay any attention to the sign-up sheet — or to where he was going.

"Ouch, that's my foot you just stepped on!" a girl cried out angrily. The girl had wavy auburn hair pulled off her face with a shiny gold barrette. She wore long dangly earrings, a pink silk shirt, and very strong lemon-scented perfume. She looked about Jessie's age. Before Benny could apologize, she hurried away.

"Mother, that little boy just stepped on my foot," the girl spoke loudly to an older woman with short blonde hair. "Thanks to him, one of my new shoes is all dirty." She held out her leg to show a smudged pink suede shoe. Several people turned around to look. Benny felt his face turn bright red.

"Oh, Melody, I can buy you new shoes in the same color," the girl's mother answered. She glared in Benny's direction, then took Melody by the arm and went up the stairs.

"I tried to say I was sorry," Benny whispered to Jessie, "but she walked away too fast."

"Don't worry, Benny." Jessie patted her brother on the arm. "I'm sure you didn't mean to step on her foot."

The Aldens and Soo Lee followed the others up the winding staircase. They walked down the hall to a big room with floor-to-ceiling windows.

A thin man with blond hair sat in the center of a circle. People holding scripts were seated around him reading their lines.

"Look, they've already started," Benny whispered loudly to Jessie.

"No they haven't, they're just practicing," said a tall, brown-haired woman who introduced herself as Nancy Wu, the stage manager. She held all the sign-up sheets in one hand. "Would those trying out for Dorothy, the Scarecrow, the Tinman, and the Cowardly Lion please come around this table," she announced.

"Why are they auditioning so many parts at once?" Violet asked her sister.

Before Jessie could answer, the blond man stood up and introduced himself as James Maynard, the director. Violet noticed he had big dark circles under his eyes.

"I'm asking all those interested in lead roles to audition together," the director was saying, "because I want to see how well you read with one another. You all know, of course, you may not get the part you try out for. You can't all be Dorothy," he said looking at the ten girls clustered around him. "But if you read well, I may assign you another part."

"I don't think I'll accept any other part but Dorothy," Melody whispered loudly to her mother. She adjusted her gold barrette as she walked with her mother to the director's table.

"You know, Mr. Maynard, my daughter has been receiving private voice lessons for the past five years," Melody's mother explained. "She's also been taking ballet for her posture."

James Maynard ran his hand through his hair and nodded politely. "Please call me Jim," was all he said.

Jessie seated herself at the long table near Melody. She noticed Sarah coming toward them and waved, but Sarah seemed lost in thought. She didn't even notice Jessie until she sat down.

"Oh, hello! You're the one I met outside the bookstore," Sarah said. She even smiled a little. The man in the tin costume joined them along with several other male and female actors who were all from the town.

"I didn't know there were so many actors in Greenfield," Henry said to Violet as he sat down to watch the auditions. The Aldens and Soo Lee made sure they sat very close to the big table so they could hear everything Jessie said.

"I recognize some of them," Violet answered. "Isn't that woman over there Mrs. Adams, the librarian?" Violet pointed to a tall woman with masses of curly blonde hair who was auditioning for the part of the Good Witch, Glinda.

Henry nodded. "Yes, you're right." He sounded a little surprised.

Since so many girls were trying out for Dorothy, the director decided to audition only the "Dorothys" first. He had the other actors stand by and watch, along with friends and relatives.

"To play the role of Dorothy, you'll have to do some dancing and singing," Jim was saying. "I hope you came prepared with a song to sing for us." The girls all nodded. The director then picked a scene from the play and asked each girl in turn to read that scene with him.

Two girls Jessie didn't know read first and second. Jessie didn't think they did well at all. The director must not have thought so either because he didn't even ask them to sing.

When it was Melody's turn, she stood up.

She didn't even use the script. She knew all her lines from memory. She moved her arms, her feet, her whole body. She sang with a beautiful, well-trained voice and when she finished, some people clapped — Melody's mother loudest of all. Jim smiled a little absentmindedly and motioned to the next girl to continue the scene.

Jessie took a deep breath when the director pointed to her. She read the part where Dorothy first meets the Scarecrow on the Yellow Brick Road. She pretended she was in the strange world of Oz holding her dog, Toto, in her arms.

James Maynard sat in front of Jessie, reading the Scarecrow's lines. When he moved his hands to brush the hair from his face, Jessie imagined him adjusting his ragged, pointy black hat, just like in the movie.

When she finished, her family applauded and cheered. Some others joined in. Jim chuckled. "Thank you, Jessie, that was well done." Jessie smiled and leaned back in her chair to listen to the others.

When Sarah began to read, the room became very still. After a few lines, Jessie sat spellbound. Sarah made Jessie see Dorothy as she really was — a little girl stranded in a strange land with only her dog for company.

For the first time that morning, no one could be heard whispering or rustling scripts. When Sarah sang her song, Jessie noticed Melody pouting. But Jim Maynard's eyes shone, and for once he sat perfectly still.

For a few seconds after Sarah stopped, there was silence. Then everyone began to applaud. Some even stood up and cheered. Sarah looked very pleased until she glanced at her watch. "Oh, no, I didn't realize how late it was getting," she muttered softly.

"Oh, do you have to go?" Melody asked, looking pleased.

Sarah turned a little pale. "No, not right away," she answered.

"Good," Jim said. He looked at Sarah closely. "I'd like you to stay to read with the other actors. I also want you to do some simple dance steps on stage this afternoon."

Sarah nodded.

Melody turned her back on Sarah and began whispering to the girl in a white frilly shirt sitting next to her.

"All right, let's continue," Jim said briskly.

Jessie barely listened to the other girls' tryouts. No one could compete with Sarah for the lead, that was sure.

"I don't see why we have to sit here while you audition all these girls!" An angry man interrupted Jessie's daydreaming. "It's a waste of our time!"

"The auditions for Dorothy are almost finished." Jim sighed and glanced at his clipboard. He turned in his chair to face the angry man. "We'll begin the auditions for the other major roles as soon as some of these girls take a short break, Mr. White."

To Jessie's surprise, Jim asked her to come back after the break to read with the adults. He invited Sarah, Melody, and two other girls to come, too.

Jessie's family crowded around her. "Jessie

you were great," Henry said proudly.

"We're staying for the rest of the auditions," Benny said. "We want to be here when you get the part."

"They won't announce the results until late tomorrow afternoon," Jessie said, laughing. Mr. Maynard has a lot of people to cast. But I'm glad you're staying. I should be finished soon." She hurried back to the table.

The man in the tin costume sat next to Jessie. He introduced himself as Harold Carlton. Of all the adult actors, he was the best by far. The director must have thought so, too, because anytime Harold read, Jim leaned back in his chair and smiled.

The impatient man, Richard White, was reading the lines for the Wizard. He stopped for a moment to mop his forehead with a handkerchief. "It's too warm in here," he complained. "Can't you tell them to turn down the heat?"

"The janitors aren't here today. We can leave a note for them," Jim answered wearily.

"You must be awfully hot with that tin helmet on all the time," Richard continued, turning to Harold. "Why don't you take it off?"

"That's not in the script," Harold joked.

Jim shrugged. "A good actor performs even when he's uncomfortable."

"I see," Richard said irritably. But he continued reading in his loud, booming voice.

"I must admit he's got the right voice for the Wizard," Sarah whispered softly to Jessie. "It's too bad about his personality."

Jessie giggled. Sarah smiled back at her, but Jessie noticed she kept looking at her watch. As time passed, Sarah grew more and more fidgety.

When they were in the middle of the scene with the Wicked Witch of the West, the stage manager interrupted.

"Excuse me, Jim, but there's a phone call for you."

Jim frowned. "Who is it?" he asked.

"A man," the stage manager answered. "He wouldn't give his name, but he said it was important."

Jim pressed his hands together and sighed. "I'll be right back," he told the actors. But he was gone more than fifteen minutes. When he returned, he looked pale.

"That was a crank call," he said slowly. "Whoever it was told me not to direct this show. If I did, there would be trouble." Jim nervously twirled the pencil in his hands.

The actors all looked up from their scripts. Some seemed puzzled, others scared.

"Oh, it's probably just a dumb joke," Jim said, but the others could tell he was worried. "Anyway, let's continue, shall we?" He sat down in his big chair and took up the script.

Sarah, after another look at her watch and at the clock in the back of the room, stood up. "I really have to go now. May I be excused?"

"Well yes, if you must," Jim told her. "But I don't like performers to leave in the middle of a scene. The auditions for the lead roles should be over in another hour, and I did want to see if you can dance."

Sarah gasped and turned pale. "Oh, I *can't* stay any longer today. Really I *can't*."

"Why not?" Melody asked loudly.

Sarah didn't answer. Instead, she bit her

lip and looked at the floor. She looked as if she were about to burst into tears.

"All right," Jim said gently, giving Sarah a puzzled look. "You can go. We may call you back tomorrow." Sarah nodded, grabbed her purple coat, and rushed out the door.

Everyone else around the table looked at one another.

"I think it's rude she didn't even wait for the others to finish," Melody whispered loudly. The girl in the frilly white shirt nodded.

Jim sighed. "All right, let's continue, shall we? Melody, why don't you read Dorothy's lines."

Melody tossed her head and began reading. Jessie tried to concentrate on her lines as she read the part of the Cowardly Lion, but she couldn't stop thinking about Sarah. Though Jessie did not want to admit it, she wondered whether Sarah had anything to do with the mysterious phone call.

CHAPTER 3

A Cast of Characters

"Why don't we go to the park for a late lunch?" Henry suggested the next day. "This way we can be nearby when the results are posted."

Soo Lee yawned and stretched her arms. She had spent the night with her cousins on a cot in Violet's room. "What is there to eat in the park?" she asked.

Henry smiled at the little girl. "Grandfather gave me some money. We can buy lunch things at the grocery store on the way over."

"That sounds good. I want peanut butter," Benny said.

"Me, too," Soo Lee agreed.

Benny put on his navy-blue jacket. "Why don't we take Watch with us? Once Jim sees all he can do, he'll give him Toto's part right away."

The others laughed. "It wouldn't hurt to take him for a walk in the park," Jessie said.

"Come here, boy. I hope you remember all the tricks I taught you," Benny said. Watch held his paw up to shake Benny's hand. Benny shook it and clipped on Watch's red leash.

"Jessie, did I tell you the stage manager said I could be an errand boy? And Soo Lee can help me," Benny said.

Jessie laughed as she walked out the front door. "Yes, Benny, you did tell me."

"Now we really can all work together," Benny continued. "We may even have a mystery to solve again."

"Yes, if that phone call was for real, we sure will," Henry said. He stopped at the corner to wait for the light.

"Remember," Jessie reminded her brothers. "I don't have a part yet."

"Oh, you will," Henry said. "We heard what the director said when you finished reading. He didn't say 'that was well done' to anyone else."

"Except Sarah," Jessie walked quickly to keep up with Henry. "He was so impressed with her, he didn't know what to say."

"I just hope Melody doesn't get a part," Benny said as he caught up with Jessie and Henry. "I wouldn't want to spend the next month working with her."

"I don't know Benny, she might," Jessie answered. "She has a very good voice."

"So does the man in the tin costume," Violet said. "I heard him practicing."

"I wonder why he never wants to take his costume off," Benny said as he held open the door to the deli.

"He must like his costume very much," Soo Lee said.

The Aldens bought chicken salad, potato chips, apples, small cartons of orange juice, rye bread, slices of a chocolate layer cake Soo

Lee admired, and paper plates. "You have a sweet tooth just like Benny," Henry teased his cousin.

As the Aldens walked toward the park, they noticed Richard White farther down the street. He stopped at a store window to admire his reflection.

"Boy, he's stuck up," Henry muttered to Violet.

Violet nodded as the children all crossed the street to the park.

The Aldens settled themselves on the stone benches near the Community Playhouse, and carefully made their sandwiches. An actress they had met the day before walked by and smiled. "The results should be posted soon," she said.

Benny swallowed a bite of his apple. "Maybe we should go see," he suggested.

Soo Lee looked longingly at the slices of chocolate layer cake. Jessie smiled at her. "We can wait until you've had your cake. The results probably aren't posted this early."

"That's fine with me." Benny grinned.

"We thought it would be." Henry tickled his brother playfully in the ribs. Benny laughed. "Don't do that while I'm eating," he protested.

"Okay, I'll wait until you're finished," Henry promised, reaching for a slice of cake.

"Well, I'm glad you're finding something to laugh about," a girl said. Benny looked up from his plate and swallowed.

"Melody?" he said surprised.

Melody's eyes and nose were puffy and red. Benny was afraid Melody would yell at him again, but to his relief she ignored him and turned to Jessie.

"I didn't get the part of Dorothy," Melody said angrily. "How could Jim give the best part to that rude girl who wouldn't even wait for the rest of us to finish?"

"Sarah has the part of Dorothy?" Jessie asked. She wasn't at all surprised. "So, the results are posted," she said more loudly.

Melody sniffed and dabbed her eyes with a pink tissue. "Yes, they want me to be the Scarecrow, but I haven't decided whether or not I'll even act in this dopey play." Melody gulped. "It would serve them right if I just left."

"We should go see the results," Henry said, paying no attention to Melody. He gathered the remains of the picnic in a paper bag and walked away. Melody stared after him and blew her nose.

"I really wish she hadn't gotten a part," Benny muttered as the Aldens entered the Playhouse. Inside, several people clustered around a bulletin board on the far wall.

"Henry, you're the tallest, why don't you see if you can read it?" Jessie suggested. She suddenly felt as if she had butterflies in her stomach.

Soon Henry rejoined his family. He was all smiles. "Jessie," he said proudly, "you have the part of the Cowardly Lion."

"Oh, Jessie, that's my favorite character in the whole play!" Benny patted his sister on the back.

"You'll have a much better costume than if you were Dorothy." Violet grinned, thinking of the fun she'd have making Jessie a furry suit with a long lion's tail.

"I've been assigned to work on scenery and lighting. You're to work on costumes, Violet. We have a meeting with the stage manager this afternoon," Henry said.

"What about me and Soo Lee?" Benny asked.

"You're down as a 'gofer,' Benny," answered Henry.

"What?" Benny raised his eyebrows.

"That means you run errands for the director. He might ask you to deliver packages or messages."

"That sounds like an important job." Benny stood up, proudly.

"Soo Lee is going to help with scenery," Henry continued.

Soo Lee smiled. "That's good."

"And when the play opens, Soo Lee, they want you to be one of the ushers." Soo Lee looked at Henry.

"An usher is someone who shows people to their seats," Henry explained. Soo Lee nodded.

"Who got the part of the Wizard?" Jessie asked.

"Richard," Henry answered. "Harold is the Tinman."

"Look, he's over there." Benny nudged Jessie. "And he's *still* wearing his tin costume. Isn't that funny?"

"What about Toto?" Jessie asked her brother.

"That part is still open. This may be Watch's big chance." Henry smiled, thinking of Watch on the stage.

"What are we waiting for?" Benny asked. "We need to get Watch an audition."

"They also need someone to play Aunty Em, Dorothy's aunt," Henry added.

Jessie was quiet a moment. "You know, Mrs. McGregor would be a wonderful Aunty Em," she said slowly. "She even knows most of the lines after helping me for my audition."

"That's a wonderful idea, Jessie," Violet said.

"Do you think she'd do it?" Henry wondered.

"It wouldn't hurt to ask her. Why don't we call her right now?" Jessie suggested.

Henry fished in his pockets for some change, as they all walked to a phone booth. "I'll call," Violet offered. The others crowded around as she put the change into the phone.

At first Mrs. McGregor sounded a little flustered at the thought of acting on the stage, but Violet finally convinced her to come down to the Playhouse and meet the director.

"She'll be here in a few minutes," Violet said as she hung up the phone. "She's driving."

"I'll go get Jim and tell him about Mrs. McGregor and Watch," Jessie said.

When Mrs. McGregor arrived, the children could tell she was pleased even though she kept saying she couldn't really act.

"We'll see about that," Jim said. He picked a scene for her to read and had Jessie read Dorothy's lines.

"Just pretend you're practicing with Jessie again at the kitchen table," Henry suggested.

Mrs. McGregor nodded and began to read. The children could tell Jim liked her voice.

When he told Mrs. McGregor she had the part, she beamed.

"You're becoming a real acting family," Jim said. He liked the Aldens. "Even your dog has a part."

"Hooray!" Benny almost shouted. "Did you audition him?"

Jim laughed. "Not really. I just watched him with Jessie. I just hope when he's on stage, he'll follow Dorothy around and not the Cowardly Lion."

"We can train him," Benny said. He felt sure Watch could do anything. He patted the dog's head. "You're such a good dog, Watch."

Watch barked and wagged his tail. Everyone laughed.

Jim looked at his watch. "It's almost time for our cast meeting in the auditorium." He nodded to Mrs. McGregor and Jessie. "Bring Watch to the meeting with you."

Jessie took Watch's leash from Benny. "I think we better put this on him," she said.

"The crew has a meeting with Nancy Wu backstage," Jim told the others. "She's going

to give you a tour and get you started on
your assignments."

"I guess we're crew, Soo Lee," Benny said.
Together, they followed Henry and Violet
backstage.

"Henry and Stuart will be working on
lighting," Nancy Wu was saying during the
backstage tour. She nodded toward Henry
and an older boy named Stuart. Then she
motioned toward the large gray panel that
had numerous controls and switches.

"This lighting board controls all the lights
used during the play," Nancy continued.
"The rest of you must not touch this board,
or any of the lights, either. That's very important." Nancy made sure everyone was lis-
tening before she continued.

"Okay, this way," she directed, as she
pulled a thick electrical cord out of the way.
The crew walked past the lighting board and
down three steps. Piles of wooden planks and
rolls of canvas were stacked along the gray
walls of the large backstage area. "We'll be
building the sets here," Nancy said.

"Have the sets been designed?" Violet asked shyly.

"Yes, we're using the designs from another production of *The Wizard of Oz* that Jim directed. But we still have to build the sets."

Henry looked at all the tools stacked on a shelf near the lumber. He could already tell he was going to like working on this play. He loved to build things.

"Violet, you'll be especially interested in this part of the tour." Nancy opened the door to the costume room. Dresses, pants, jackets, animal costumes, even suits of armor hung on racks, closet bars, or hooks. Shelves on one side of the room held hats, helmets, caps, and shoes in all shapes and sizes.

"Oh, some of these costumes are so beautiful!" Violet stepped into the room so she could see some of the dresses better. She gently touched the sleeve of a long red velvet gown.

The group continued up three steps to the other side of the stage. The crew could hear some of the performers rehearsing behind the curtain. All of a sudden, a loud shriek could be heard from every corner of the auditorium.

"They must be rehearsing the tornado scene," Henry suggested.

Nancy shook her head. "There isn't a scream like that anywhere in this script."

Now they recognized Melody's voice. "Look what you did," Melody was saying very loudly. "I won't act with someone so clumsy! I bet you made me fall on purpose."

The children looked at one another. "I might have known it was Melody who screamed," Nancy said.

"Should we see if we can help?" Henry asked.

Nancy shook her head. The crew could hear the voice of the director and Sarah's voice trying to calm Melody.

"Don't come near me," Melody yelled before she burst into tears and rushed off-stage. Jim came after her. Some of the other performers followed, including Jessie and Sarah.

"What happened?" Violet asked Jessie.

"Melody fell when she was practicing the

dance the Scarecrow does with Dorothy. She's blaming Sarah."

"Is she hurt?" Violet asked.

"I don't think so." Jessie shook her head. "In fact, I don't think Sarah even touched Melody."

In the meantime, Melody had found a phone backstage.

"Mom," Melody said. "I need you to come pick me up right away. Something *awful* has happened."

Jim sighed and looked at Nancy. "I think we've done enough for today. I'll see all the performers tomorrow."

"You might not see *me*!" Melody said angrily as she hung up the receiver. "My mother will probably want to talk to you."

Jim ignored her. "You all have the rehearsal schedules. We'll be practicing almost every day." The director turned away without waiting for anyone to answer. He looked even more tired than yesterday.

Nancy quickly gave the crew last-minute instructions about their various jobs. She expected them tomorrow as well.

The Aldens left Melody sitting on the couch in the dressing room. As they walked through the main lobby, Jessie gasped.

The large poster listing the results of the audition was torn. Someone had crossed Sarah's name off the list. In pink crayon, these words were written next to her name:

Don't Go On With The Show !

Henry and Soo Lee stared at the sign. Violet asked shakily, "Has Sarah seen this?"

"I don't know," Jessie said, looking around. "I think she left through the backstage door while Melody was calling her mother."

"Could Melody have written this?" Benny asked.

"She likes pink," Soo Lee said.

Benny said, "I hadn't thought of that!"

Suddenly, Jim strode into the lobby with Nancy at his heels. He stopped when he saw the note and gave a low whistle. "Who did this?" he exclaimed.

"We don't know," Henry answered.

Jim and Nancy exchanged glances. "Melody?" Jessie suggested. "She's so jealous of

Sarah for getting the lead role."

"Maybe," Jim said slowly, but he didn't sound convinced. "But when could she have done it? She was on stage all evening."

"That's true," Henry said, nodding.

"I'll have to talk to Melody and some of the other performers personally," Jim said frowning.

He turned to the Aldens. "Can I count on you not to say anything until I've gotten to the bottom of this?"

They nodded solemnly.

"Good. I'll let you know what happens," Jim said. "Right now, I don't want to upset the rest of the cast and crew." He pressed his fingers to his forehead.

"Most people left the building through the door backstage. We're probably the only ones who have seen it," Jessie said, trying to make Jim feel better.

"There must be an explanation," Henry said. "Whoever wrote this note may be the same person who threatened Jim yesterday on the phone. Somebody, somewhere, doesn't want this show to go on."

CHAPTER 4

Behind the Scenes

"I still think Melody had something to do with that note," Benny said the next day. Benny and Soo Lee were backstage, with many others, sanding boards for the scenery.

Soo Lee took some more sandpaper. "I don't know, Benny," she said.

Violet came out of the costume room holding the furry yellow-brown material she was using to make Jessie's lion costume. "Did Melody come back after that scene last night?"

Benny nodded. "She's on stage right now rehearsing with Jessie and Harold."

"She's limping, too," Soo Lee said.

"How do you know?" Benny asked his cousin.

"I saw her in the wings," Soo Lee said.

"I bet she's just *pretending* to limp." Benny did not sound at all sorry. "She wants everyone to feel sorry for her."

Violet threaded her needle and sat on a chair next to Benny and Soo Lee. "It's too bad Jessie has to spend so much time with her on stage," she said.

"Oh, there you are," Benny suddenly called out to Henry as he saw Henry coming toward them. Benny proudly pointed to his smoothly sanded board.

"That's good, Benny." Henry smiled, but he soon looked serious again. "Jim told me he spoke to Melody last night."

"What did he say?" Benny held his piece of sandpaper in midair.

"He told her if she kept interrupting rehearsals, he didn't want her in the play."

Benny's eyes grew wider. "Did he ask her about the note in pink crayon?"

Henry nodded. "He said she seemed just as surprised about it as we were."

"She's a good actress," Benny reminded his brother.

"I agree," Henry said. "But we shouldn't jump to any conclusions. Let's just watch her — closely." The others nodded.

Jim suddenly came backstage. Everyone stopped talking and looked at him. "Has anyone seen Sarah?" he asked.

Henry, Soo Lee, and Benny shook their heads.

"What! You mean she hasn't shown up yet?" Nancy looked at her watch. She was busy sketching the design for Oz's palace on a big piece of canvas. When the canvas painting was finished, it would be mounted on the wooden frame Henry, Benny, and Soo Lee were building.

"No, no one's seen her." Jim looked worried. "I can't have this. I can't have the major performers being this late. She was supposed to be here almost an hour ago."

"Maybe she's been delayed on the bus," Violet suggested.

Jim stared at Violet. "If Sarah comes in, tell her I want to see her right away," he announced.

"We will." Violet said.

"Okay," Jim announced. "I'd like to rehearse the scene with the Munchkins. Could I have all the Munchkins on stage, please." Several children and short adults followed the director.

Stuart rushed by carrying a large white extension cord. "Oh, there you are, Henry," he said. "I want to show you how to work the lights during the tornado scene."

"I'm coming." Henry stood up and brushed the sawdust off his pants.

Benny looked at the activity around him. The actress who played the Wicked Witch of the West was mixing paint for the scenery. The Good Witch, who was being played by Mrs. Adams, the town librarian, sewed the hem of her beautiful gown. The Wizard,

Richard, hammered boards together to make Dorothy's house.

"You have a lot of actors working backstage," Benny said.

"Oh, yes," Nancy answered him cheerfully from across the large room. "Everyone does something to help out in community theater."

"Ouch!" Richard suddenly yelled and dropped his hammer. "You can tell Jim I am *not*, and I repeat *not working on scenery any longer!* I'm an actor, not a carpenter."

"Oh, Richard," Nancy said, shaking her head.

Richard stood up and glared. "I think I'll go see what they're doing with the lights for my scenes," he announced.

Nancy sighed and stood up to stretch. She walked over to where the Aldens were working. Violet was carefully cutting into the furry yellow-brown material. Every once in a while, she paused to look at the sketch she'd made for the lion costume. Nancy looked over her shoulder.

"I wonder what could have happened to Sarah," Violet said.

Nancy didn't answer right away. She was too busy looking at Violet's sketch. "Violet," she finally said, "that's really good. We should have you design the costumes for the Scarecrow and Wizard, too."

"Oh, I'd love to," Violet said eagerly, looking up from her cutting.

"Wait until I tell Mrs. Adams. She's the other person making costumes," Nancy explained.

"You mean the one who's playing the Good Witch?" Violet sounded pleased. She liked Mrs. Adams.

"Yes." Nancy chuckled a little. "She was worried about having so many costumes to make in such a short time. I can't wait to tell her we have another pro on the crew."

Violet felt her cheeks flush. "Thank you," she said, looking at the floor.

Jessie came backstage holding her script. "Benny, Jim would like you to come on stage and hold Watch. The stage lights are getting him very excited."

Benny nodded and stood up. At that moment Sarah rushed in through the stage door.

"Where were you?" Nancy snapped. "You should have been here at three o'clock."

"I know." Sarah hurriedly took off her purple coat and hung it near the costume room. "I was looking for my script. I couldn't find it anywhere." Sarah looked as if she were near tears. "I know I had it yesterday."

Nancy sighed. "What else can go wrong?" she whispered to herself. "You can borrow mine for now." She handed Sarah her well-worn script. "But be careful with it. It's all marked up with my notes."

"I will," Sarah said solemnly as she took the script. Violet noticed Sarah's eyes looked a little red.

"We can probably find you another script." Nancy's voice softened. "I'll look around for one while you're rehearsing. Now go on. Jim wants to see you right away."

Sarah nodded and rummaged through her big black shoulder bag for another tissue before she hurried on stage. Jessie and Benny followed behind her.

Nancy went to the costume room to tell Mrs. Adams about Violet. All was quiet, until Melody came backstage limping rather noticeably. She sat down on the stairs.

"There's nothing to do — only Sarah and the Munchkins are rehearsing now," she said crossly. "You know . . ." She paused, waiting for Violet to look up from her sewing. "I think I sprained my ankle when I fell last night."

"Did you see a doctor?" Violet asked politely.

"Yes, he told me it wasn't sprained. But he gave me some medicine to help numb the pain."

Violet nodded. She was glad when Nancy and Mrs. Adams called Violet into the costume room.

"Oh, Violet, I would like to introduce you to Mrs. Adams."

"Oh, I know Violet from the library." Mrs. Adams held out her hand. "Nancy's been telling me how well you sew."

"You should show her your sketch," Nancy said to Violet as she rummaged through the bottom drawer in the big dresser. Suddenly she stopped and looked puzzled. Quickly, she opened the other drawers and looked through them.

"Oh, no! Oh, my goodness!" Nancy almost shrieked.

"What's wrong?" Mrs. Adams asked in her soft voice.

"All the props I collected yesterday are missing!" Nancy wrung her hands. She looked at Violet. "Did you move them?" she asked.

Violet shook her head. "I didn't even know they were there," she said.

"Neither did I," Mrs. Adams said. "What was in that drawer?"

Nancy put her hands in front of her face. "Dorothy's red shoes, your wand, and the Tinman's ax."

"Those things can all be replaced," Mrs. Adams assured Nancy. "I can make another wand, and I also have a pair of red shoes that should fit Sarah."

"I can make a cardboard ax," Violet said, looking around the large costume room.

Everything seemed to be the way she'd left it earlier. "Maybe we should check to see if anything else is missing," she suggested.

"Good idea." Nancy nodded. "There's probably a logical explanation for this. When rehearsal is over, I'll talk to Jim. Maybe he took the props."

Violet opened the narrow top drawer. It held makeup, cotton balls, and lotions. Scarves, sweaters, pencils, crayons, drawing paper, and boards filled the other drawers.

"Everything seems to be in order," Nancy said, looking over Violet's shoulder. Mrs. Adams opened the door of a wardrobe. "I put the material for Dorothy's pinafore in here," she explained. Suddenly she gasped.

Violet and Nancy were quickly by her side. The blue-and-white checked material had been ripped to shreds!

CHAPTER 5

A Role for Watch

On stage, Benny was having trouble controlling Watch. The dog kept running to Jessie who stood in the wings waiting for her cue to come on. Watch wouldn't pay any attention to Sarah.

Jim was shaking his head. "This may not work," he told Benny. "Take him off the stage so we can get on with this." He looked at his watch. "Maybe, if we finish rehearsing early, you can take him outside with Sarah so he can get used to her."

Benny nodded and grabbed his dog's collar. As he walked Watch backstage, Benny did a little dance similar to the one he'd just seen the Munchkins rehearse. He didn't know that Jim was watching, smiling.

"Okay," Jim said, turning to the Munchkins on stage. "Why don't you start again from the beginning?"

The Munchkins began their little dance welcoming Dorothy to their country. Jim watched them for a few moments. "No, stop. You're not in step with one another." The director shook his head and climbed up on stage.

"Look," he said taking one of the Munchkins by the hand. "You need to start by raising your left foot, then the right. Now, start again."

The Munchkins obeyed. Jim seemed deep in thought. "Stop," he called again. "We need another Munchkin to fill out this middle row. Benny, where are you?" Jim looked around.

Benny stood in the wings holding Watch by the collar. "Sit, boy," he said before he went on stage.

"You seem to catch on quickly," Jim said, smiling at Benny. "I'd like to give you a small role as a Munchkin. Would you like that?"

Benny nodded, pleased.

"Okay," Jim said. "Stand here, Benny. Now take it from the top," Jim called to the others.

"What?" Benny whispered to the Munchkin girl next to him.

"That means start at the beginning," she whispered back.

Just then Nancy came out to talk to Jim. She looked terribly upset.

"What?" Jim almost shouted after Nancy said a few sentences. "Ask everybody to come out on stage!"

Jim paced until all the cast and crew members had assembled. He told them about the missing props, the ripped costume, and the note written on the board yesterday.

"Are you suggesting one of *us* is responsible?" Richard asked.

"I'm just trying to get to the bottom of this." Jim sounded very angry. "I will not have the show ruined by a lot of nonsense!"

Jim did not look at Melody when he spoke, but several others did.

"We're not blaming anyone," Nancy said. "But if you have any idea who might be responsible, please come talk to Jim."

"Yes, please," Jim pleaded. "I'll keep whatever you tell me in confidence."

"What does that mean?" Soo Lee tapped Violet on the arm.

"That means he won't tell anyone," Violet answered.

"All right. Go back to your jobs backstage. Rehearsal's over for tonight. Tomorrow, we'll have a piano player here. I want you to have your lines memorized by the end of the week." Jim sounded very tired.

As the cast and crew scrambled off the stage, Jim suggested that Benny and Jessie take Watch out with Sarah. "Get Watch used to her," he advised.

The sun was setting when Watch led Sarah, Jessie, and Benny to the stone benches near the school. "He wants to chase squirrels," Jessie explained to Sarah.

Sarah laughed and stooped down to pet Watch who was straining his leash. Jessie looked at Sarah in surprise. It sounded good to hear her laugh for a change. She usually looked so serious.

"Let's find a stick before we let him loose," Jessie suggested, running ahead.

"Good idea," Benny said, hurrying to keep up with the dog. "Maybe he'll play catch with us."

Sarah threw her big shoulder bag on one of the benches and raced after the Aldens. They played with Watch until it became dark. Jessie and Benny had Sarah give Watch commands so he would become used to her voice.

"I think we're ready to go inside and tell Jim you two are getting along fine." Jessie smiled at the sight of Watch obediently trailing Sarah.

"Yes, it's getting cold out here," Sarah said as she stooped down to pick up her big shoulder bag from the bench. The bag was on its side and when Sarah reached for it, a large manila folder fell out.

Benny started to pick it up, but Sarah quickly snatched it from him. "Don't touch that," she said.

"What is it?" Benny asked, pointing at the folder as Sarah quickly shoved it in her purse.

"Oh, nothing, nothing at all," she said quickly. Without another word, she turned and hurried toward the Playhouse.

Jessie and Benny exchanged glances and followed Sarah inside. Jim was waiting for them on stage. "How did Watch do?" he asked, patting the dog on the head.

"He's really getting used to Sarah," Benny said, smiling proudly at his dog. As if in response, Watch went over to Sarah and wiggled his body. Sarah forced a smile and stooped down to pet him.

"Good," Jim said. "Watch, it looks like you still have a job."

Watch sat down by Jim's feet and wagged his tail. "He's happy," Benny said, translating for his dog.

"I'm glad someone is," Jim said. "See you tomorrow. By the way, the rest of your family has already gone home. Better hurry to be in time for your dinner." Jim actually smiled.

"Would you like to come to our house for dinner?" Jessie asked Sarah as they were all walking out the door with Watch.

Sarah looked down at the ground and played with the purple belt on her wool coat. "No, thank you," she mumbled, shaking her head. "I have to go."

Jessie was very puzzled by Sarah's behavior. She'd seemed so friendly only a few minutes ago.

"I wonder what Sarah has in that envelope," Jessie said thoughtfully as she hurried home with Benny. She wrapped her red scarf more tightly around her neck.

"Maybe it was the missing script," Jessie said. "Maybe Sarah hadn't really lost it."

"I don't know," Benny said. "But whatever it was, it was addressed to New York City and she sure didn't want us to see it."

CHAPTER 6

A Familiar Face?

"Benny, what are you going to use that star for?" Violet asked a few days later. Benny was at the kitchen table. He had glue, scissors, cardboard, and a small pile of shiny gold paper spread in front of him.

"I'm making Watch a gold star for his doghouse." Benny carefully cut out the cardboard star Violet had drawn for him.

Violet smiled. "Watch has been doing well in rehearsal."

"Yes." Benny nodded. "Nothing's gone wrong for a few days. Jim doesn't even yell as much anymore." Benny continued cutting the cardboard.

"Grandfather is taking us all out to dinner," Violet told Benny.

"Really!" Benny exclaimed. He put down his scissors. "I hope we're going to the pizzeria."

"If that's where you want to go, Benny, the pizzeria it will be," Grandfather said as he came into the kitchen. "Are you ready to leave soon?"

"I *am* sort of hungry," Benny admitted.

At dinner, Benny ordered two slices of his favorite pizza — pepperoni with special tomato sauce and lots of cheese. He also asked for apple juice and a green salad.

Henry took a bite of his pizza. "You know, the man at the table by the window looks kind of familiar," he remarked.

Violet and Jessie looked sideways. "I think I've seen his picture in the paper," Jessie said. She poured some dressing on her salad.

Grandfather frowned a little. "I know I've seen him before, too," he said slowly. "I just can't remember where."

Benny reached for his glass of apple juice. "I don't know him," he said. "Oops!" Benny shouted as his glass of juice spilled onto the red-and-white checked tablecloth.

Several people in the restaurant turned toward their table, including the man who looked familiar. When he saw the Aldens, he started to nod in their direction, then suddenly stopped and turned away.

A waiter in a white apron hurried over with a wet cloth. Another waiter brought Benny a new glass of juice.

"Did you see that?" Violet asked her sister.

"What, the juice spilling?" Jessie asked.

"No." Violet shook her head. "That man who looked familiar knows us, too, I think."

Jessie turned toward the man, but he had put on his coat and was heading out the door. She shrugged. "I guess he must have finished eating," she said to Violet.

Benny took a big sip from his new glass. "This juice tastes much better," he told the waiter, who laughed.

"Enjoy the rest of your meal," the waiter said.

Soo Lee carefully put her glass of grape juice on the table. "I hope it doesn't spill," she said.

Grandfather said, "Don't worry. Oh, Soo Lee that reminds me." He turned in his chair to face her. "Alice dropped off a suitcase of clothes for you today. She said you could stay at our house until the play is over."

Soo Lee smiled happily. She liked staying with her cousins.

Benny pushed aside his empty plate. "You know," he told his family, "Watch really liked his gold star. I put it on his house before we left."

"How do you know he liked it?" Henry teased.

"Because he tried to jump up and lick it," Benny said.

Grandfather chuckled. "I hope his stardom doesn't go to his head," he remarked, as he looked proudly around the table. "You're all doing so well with this play."

"Oh, we're enjoying it," Jessie said. "It's just too bad so many funny things happened in the beginning."

"At least, Melody's been on her best behavior at rehearsals," Violet remarked.

"I've noticed that," Henry said. He poured
himself some water from the pitcher. "That
talk with Jim must have really scared her."

"You really think she's the one who made
the phone call, wrote the note, and took all
those props?" Jessie asked.

"Don't forget the ripped costume," Benny
reminded her.

"I don't know what to think," Henry said
slowly. "At first I thought Melody wanted
to give Sarah a bad time for getting the lead,
but now I'm not so sure."

"I know what you mean." Jessie played
with her spoon. "Melody seems really scared
when anything bad happens, and lately she's
tried to do her best."

"I don't think she wants to hurt the show,"
Violet agreed.

"Then *who* does?" Benny wondered.

"That's what we have to find out." Henry
said.

As the Aldens drove home from the restaurant, they passed the Community Playhouse.

"Hey, look!" Benny shouted. A bright light shone from the second floor.

"That's where the stage is. Maybe someone is practicing," Soo Lee suggested.

"So late?" Grandfather asked, looking at his watch.

"We saw Jim turn all the lights out after rehearsal. He even locked the door. No one's supposed to be in there," Violet pointed out.

"No, but someone is," Henry said.

Grandfather stopped the car and the Aldens got out. Henry tried the door, but it was locked.

"That's funny," Violet said.

"Maybe Jim or Nancy came back to check on something and forgot to turn the lights off," Jessie said.

"Well, there's nothing we can do now," Grandfather said.

"We'll tell Jim in the morning," said Henry.

"He's not going to like this," Benny added.

CHAPTER 7

Problems on the Set

"Someone noticed a light on in the theater late last night," Jim announced to the cast and crew the next day. He paused to nervously pull up the collar of his faded blue shirt.

"Are you sure it wasn't the janitor?" Richard asked.

"I was the last one in the building. I turned out all the lights and locked the door," Jim said as he paced up and down the stage.

Violet was worried about Jim. He looked paler and thinner than ever.

"Okay, let's get started," Jim called. He suddenly seemed in a hurry to begin rehearsing. "I want Sarah, Jessie, Melody, Harold, and Richard on stage."

As Benny made his way backstage, he noticed Sarah in the wings. She had a large manila folder tucked under one arm. When she noticed Benny looking at her, she quickly stuck the folder in her script.

"Did you ever find your script?" Benny asked, trying to sound friendly.

"Uh, yes. I mean no. Nancy found an extra script." Sarah seemed anxious to get away from Benny.

"I really think there should be a softer light on me in this scene," Richard was saying loudly to Henry and Jim on stage. "I see no need for a green gel."

"A what?" Benny asked Jessie.

"It's a piece of thick plastic you put over a stage light to make it change color," Jessie explained softly.

"You have to look green." Jim tried to

sound patient with Richard. "We need to have green lighting in this scene. The Wizard *does* live in the Emerald City."

"Why can't there be a soft, white spotlight on me?" Richard demanded.

"Look, I give the lighting directions here," Jim said firmly. "Now, please take your positions so we can get on with this scene."

"Come on, Benny, you should be backstage," Henry called softly. He pulled one of the levers on the lighting board down to low.

"I'm going," Benny said. He did a few dance steps from his Munchkin routine.

"You're showing off," Henry teased him.

"Not as much as Richard is," Benny pointed out. Henry couldn't argue.

Backstage, Violet and Soo Lee were making the tail for Jessie's lion costume. Benny went over to watch them.

"Oh, Violet," Nancy called as she came into the costume room. "Could you make a big poster for the show? We open in a week and we need more advertising." Nancy sighed and looked at the jumble of materials spread out on the big table in front of the girls.

"I can make the poster right here. Remember, we found lots of crayons and paints in this drawer." Violet opened the long thin drawer of the black dresser.

"Good, I know you'll do a good job. All you Aldens are such a big help around here," Nancy said, looking appreciatively at Benny and Soo Lee. "By the way, Benny, if you're not busy, I'd like you to help Mrs. McGregor paint the Yellow Brick Road on the backdrop. I have to be in the wings all afternoon to give the actors their cues."

"I'm coming," Benny said cheerfully. He liked to paint.

When Violet had sketched and painted the poster, she left it on the table in the costume room so the paint would dry. Then she went with Soo Lee to help Benny finish painting the Yellow Brick Road.

"Oh, good, I'm glad you're here to help." Mrs. McGregor brushed a wisp of hair off her forehead with her arm. "Benny has to go on stage now. They're rehearsing the Munchkin scene."

As she worked on the Yellow Brick Road, Violet noticed people going in and out of the costume room. When Richard came out, Violet asked, "Can I help you?"

"Oh, no." Richard sounded a little embarrassed. "I, uh, was just looking for my costume."

"It's hanging on a hook near the wardrobe," Violet said as she dabbed yellow paint on the big canvas backdrop in front of her.

"Yes, I saw it." Richard played nervously with his bow tie. "It's too bad I have to wear a brown suit during most of the play when all the others have such colorful costumes."

"You have a colorful part," Mrs. McGregor reminded him.

"Well, yes," Richard admitted. "But a brighter suit would make me stand out more in the Emerald City."

Violet didn't know what to say. She nodded a little and continued painting. By the time rehearsal was over, the Yellow Brick Road was finished.

"Tomorrow, after the paint dries, they'll put the canvas on the big wooden frame Henry made," Mrs. McGregor said.

Before she left, Violet went to the costume room to get her coat. She carefully checked all the costumes. Mrs. Adams had made Dorothy a new blue-checked pinafore, and it hung crisply on a hook. The Lion and Scarecrow costumes lay finished on one of the tables. Nothing had been touched.

Violet breathed a sigh of relief, until she looked for the poster. It was missing!

"What's the matter?" Nancy asked as she came into the costume room behind Violet. Violet's eyes were very wide.

"The poster I made is gone!" Violet's voice shook a little.

"It has to be somewhere," Nancy pointed out. She began to look in the closet and under the table. "Did you notice anyone coming into the costume room when you were painting scenery?"

Violet frowned. "Well, yes," she said. "Richard."

Nancy nodded.

"And other people came in and out," Violet continued, "but I didn't pay much attention."

Nancy sighed. "I'm going to look for the poster backstage, then I'll make an announcement. Maybe someone already hung it outside."

"No, I don't think so," a shrill voice said behind them. Melody had silently slipped into the room wearing her pink ballet slippers. She waved her hands in front of her to show off her purple nail polish.

Nancy and Violet stared at her in surprise.

"What do you mean, you don't think so?" Nancy asked. "Have you seen the poster?"

"Why, isn't it over there?" Melody pointed with her purple-nailed index finger.

The poster stood in the far corner of the room facing the wall. Violet examined it carefully. Everything looked all right except someone had tried to make the letters in Richard's name bigger!

"Of all the nerve!" Nancy exclaimed.

Violet stared at her poster in silence. "I think I can fix it," she said after a few moments. "I'll just have to make Sarah's name a little bigger, too."

Nancy just shook her head. "I'm going to have to have a talk with Richard." She hurried out of the room.

Melody paid no attention to the conversation between Nancy and Violet. "I want to see my Scarecrow costume," she insisted. "Now."

"It's right here." Violet pointed to the patchwork jumpsuit filled with cotton and straw.

"It looks so itchy," Melody complained.

Violet sighed. "It shouldn't be," she answered. "The straw won't be touching your skin."

"I wish I could wear one of these long dresses," Melody said as she inspected one of the long pink silk gowns hanging on the rack.

"Melody?" Violet asked. "How did you know where the poster was?"

Melody played with one of the rings on

her finger. "I just saw it there when I came in earlier to change into my ballet slippers."

"Did you notice anyone fiddling with it?"

Melody held the pink gown to her body and examined her reflection in the full-length mirror. "What do you mean fiddling with it?" she asked without looking at Violet.

"I mean, did you see anyone changing the lettering on it?" Although Violet sounded polite, she was beginning to lose her patience.

"No." Melody shook her long auburn curls. "The poster was just sitting there against the wall. I didn't touch it, if that's what you mean. Why would I want to make Richard's name bigger?"

Melody twirled in front of the mirror one more time before hanging the dress back on the rack. She left the room without saying another word to Violet.

When Nancy came back, she looked discouraged. "Richard's left for the evening. I promise you, I'll talk to him tomorrow."

Violet sighed. "I think I'll finish this poster at home. I have lots of paints there."

"Don't stay up too late," Nancy advised as she put on her coat. "You'll need your energy for all those costume fittings tomorrow."

"I won't," Violet assured her as she gathered her things to leave.

As the Aldens walked out of the Community Playhouse, they noticed a big white car pulled up in front of the building. A man in a tweed coat sat behind the wheel drumming his fingers on the dashboard.

"Have you seen a girl named Sarah Bellamy?" the man called to the Aldens as they walked past his car.

"Yes, we know her. She's staying late to practice her lines with Jim, the director," Jessie answered.

The man shook his head impatiently. "I can't wait here forever," he complained as he leaned on his horn and honked.

"I don't think she can hear you," Benny pointed out. The man glared in Benny's direction.

"Would one of you mind going inside to find her?" The man tried to sound polite.

"You see, I don't want to lose my parking place," he explained.

"I can go," Benny said.

"I'll go with you, Benny," said Jessie. She didn't notice any other cars parked nearby and wondered why the man was afraid of losing his parking place.

"We'll meet you at the house, then," Mrs. McGregor suggested. "I have to get dinner started, and Soo Lee and Violet are helping me. Aren't you?" she added winking at them.

"I'll help with dinner, too," Henry said as he stamped his feet a little on the pavement to keep warm. He took the poster from Violet to carry.

It took Jessie and Benny longer than they thought to walk backstage because they met some cast members in the lobby.

"Have you seen Sarah?" they asked.

"No," Mrs. Adams answered. "But she did say something a while ago about wanting to stay late for practice."

Once Jessie and Benny reached the auditorium, it was completely dark. "All the actors must have left," Benny said.

The Aldens looked in the costume room, the dressing rooms, and on the stage. Jessie even turned on the house lights so she could see the whole auditorium, but Sarah was nowhere to be found.

"She must have gone home," Jessie said finally as she turned off the lights. "Maybe she didn't know she was getting picked up."

"It's funny Jim's gone, too," Benny said. "He usually likes to stay late!"

"We seem to be the only ones here," Jessie said, looking out at the darkened auditorium.

Benny nodded. "Let's go out and tell that man we can't find Sarah," he said. "Do you think he's her father?" he added.

Jessie shrugged. "He might be. He does look a little bit like her."

"He has dark hair and blue eyes," said Benny. "Sarah does, too."

Before they left, Jessie made sure all the lights controlled by the lighting board were turned off. She took the red flashlight near the board so Benny and she could find their way to the door.

"It's dark back here," Benny said as he sidestepped a pile of lumber stacked near the wall. "I'm glad you found a flashlight."

"Yes," Jessie agreed. "I don't know why they turned the night-light off."

"Jessie!" Benny whispered loudly. He grabbed his sister's arm. "I hear voices!"

Jessie moved closer to the backstage door. "Don't worry, they're just talking outside," she whispered. "No one's backstage."

"I won't let you do this!" a man's voice said angrily.

"Do you think that's Jim?" Benny whispered. "Who's he talking to?"

Jessie put her finger to her lips and shook her head. "I can't tell," she said after a moment.

"You have to stop!" the man kept saying. The girl answered in low muffled tones.

"That's Sarah's voice!" Benny whispered. "But I can't hear what she's saying."

Benny and Jessie looked at each other. Benny's big eyes grew even rounder. "Do you think Sarah's been the one doing all those things to the props and costumes . . . ?"

"And Jim's telling her to stop?" Jessie finished the sentence for her brother. She shook her head. "It sounds that way, but we don't know for sure."

Jessie beamed the flashlight on the doorknob. "Why don't we go outside and see what's going on?" she suggested.

Suddenly the girl outside the stage door burst into tears. Jessie hesitated with her hand on the doorknob. "I don't think we should interrupt their conversation," she said finally.

Benny nodded. "Okay. We can go out the side door," he said.

Jessie turned, but something caught her eye.

"Look, Benny," she called in a low voice.

"What is it?" Benny asked.

Jessie pointed the flashlight at the backdrop of the wizard's palace. "Somebody moved it," Jessie whispered. "When we were working this afternoon on the Yellow Brick Road, I'm sure the Wizard's palace was facing the wall near those boards."

When Jessie shone the light on the Wizard's palace, the Aldens could see it was splattered with big drops of black paint. Attached to the set was a big note written in red ink.

"Can you read what it says?" Benny asked. Jessie moved her flashlight. Softly she read the note aloud. It said:

Watch out, my pretty!

CHAPTER 8

Dress Rehearsal

Jessie and Benny stared at the ruined set in horror.

"Who would do that?" asked Benny. "Can it be fixed?"

It took Jessie a few moments to answer. "Let's go find Jim," she finally said. "I hope that was his voice we heard. Maybe he's still outside."

Jessie and Benny rushed out the backstage door, but no one was in sight.

"Let's go home. We can look up Jim's phone number," Jessie suggested at last.

In the street, Jessie and Benny saw no sign of the man in the big white car.

"Maybe he found Sarah when we were backstage," Benny said to his sister as they hurried home.

Jessie nodded absentmindedly. "I can't help thinking about that conversation we overheard," Jessie said. "I just can't believe Sarah would do all those things. She's so serious about her acting — and about this show."

At home, Mrs. McGregor waited to serve dinner until Jessie and Benny could call Jim. They were surprised to find his number wasn't listed in the phone book.

"Try Nancy," Grandfather suggested.

"She's not home," Jessie said as she put down the receiver a moment later. "What are we going to do?"

"You really think the set is ruined?" Violet said sadly. She couldn't believe it.

"We might be able to touch it up, but it will never really look the same," Jessie said.

"Well, there's nothing you can do about it tonight. You've tried your best," Grandfather said gently. "Why don't we all have dinner and try to forget these problems until tomorrow."

But the Aldens could not forget. That evening, Henry, Jessie, Violet, Benny, and Soo Lee sat up late talking. They made a list of all the suspicious things that had happened. Then they tried to remember who had been backstage when anything had gone wrong. Their list of suspects included Melody, Richard, Sarah, and even the Tinman.

"After all, we've never even seen the Tinman's face," Henry said.

"He doesn't even take his tin head off to eat!" Benny added.

"Maybe we should add Melody's mother to the list?" Violet suggested.

"She hasn't really been backstage at all since the auditions," Henry reminded them. "What we really need to do now is watch these people carefully. I'd be willing to watch Richard and see what he does."

"That's a very good idea," Jessie said. "I'll take Sarah. I'm on stage with her so much anyway."

"I'll tail Melody," Violet volunteered. "She comes to the costume room a lot to complain about her Scarecrow outfit."

"That leaves Soo Lee and me with the Tinman," Benny said. "Between the two of us, we should be able to see everything he does."

First thing in the morning, the Aldens rushed to the playhouse. Nancy and Jim were already backstage. After one look at their faces, the Aldens knew they had seen the ruined set.

"We saw it like that last night and tried to call you," Jessie said. She was a little out of breath from running.

"Tell us exactly what you saw," Jim said quietly. He looked very serious.

Jessie and Benny told him all they could about the white car, the man looking for Sarah, the darkened auditorium, and the discovery of the ruined set. They even told him about the conversation they had overheard between Sarah and someone. At the mention of the conversation, Jim looked puzzled, but he didn't say anything.

At the end of the Aldens' story, Jim sighed heavily. "Well, I must have another talk with the cast," he said slowly. "In the meantime, we're going to have to redo this set."

"Violet can sketch a new palace on canvas. She's very good," Nancy said as she gave Violet a small smile. It was the first time anyone had looked happy that morning.

"I can paint it once Violet does the sketch," Henry assured Jim. "I've finished setting the lights."

Jim nodded approvingly. "Good," he said.

"Soo Lee and I can help paint, too," Benny reminded them.

"You certainly can," Nancy said. "You both did such a good job on the Yellow Brick Road."

"Okay, we all better go to work," Jim said. "We have a show to put on next week. By the way, Violet, how did the poster turn out? I want to hang it outside today."

"Oh, I finished it," Violet said shyly. She rummaged in her big canvas bag and brought it out to show Jim and Nancy.

"It's good," Jim said approvingly.

"You touched it up very well," Nancy said. "I can't tell anyone even tinkered with it."

Jim made another announcement to the cast and crew about the set and Violet's poster. No one claimed responsibility. But people became more and more nervous.

No one stayed late at night anymore. After rehearsals, people left the auditorium in groups. And no one ever wanted to be backstage alone.

For the Aldens, the next week flew by. Violet was able to sketch the Wizard's palace in a day. She didn't help paint it because she was too busy finishing the costumes and following Melody. She noticed Melody spent a lot of time practicing her lines and trying on gowns in front of the big mirror in the dressing room.

Benny, Soo Lee, and Henry did such a good job repainting the Wizard's palace that many felt it looked even better than before. Henry found it easy to keep track of Richard because he always seemed to be by the lighting board when he wasn't on stage.

"I wish Richard wouldn't bother us so much about the lighting for his scenes," Stuart complained to Henry one day when Richard was on stage.

"I know what you mean," Henry answered. "Watch out, here he comes."

Stuart groaned and rolled his eyes.

"Oh, boys," Richard boomed in his loud voice. "Could you provide some special sound effects when I leave the Wizard's palace to go back home?"

"What kind of special effects?" Henry asked, trying to sound polite.

"Perhaps you could put on a recording of a drum roll?" Richard suggested. "I think the scene where the Wizard leaves Oz is the most important one in the play, don't you?" Richard asked. He didn't look as if he expected an answer.

Henry and Stuart exchanged glances.

"I think we should talk to Jim before we get the recording," Stuart said.

Richard sighed. "Well, if you must," he answered before he was called back on stage.

Jessie, Sarah, Melody, and the Tinman all had very busy rehearsal schedules, but they helped with the scenery when they weren't on stage. The Tinman turned out to be a very good painter. Much to Benny's surprise, he kept his mask on even when he worked on the sets.

"Don't you ever take your costume off?" Benny asked one day.

The Tinman paused and dipped his brush into some blue paint. "I like to keep it on every minute I'm in the theater," he explained. "That way I always stay in character."

"You mean you always pretend to be the person you're playing on stage?" Benny looked impressed.

"Yes, that's right," the Tinman answered. Benny was almost sure the Tinman winked at him, but it was hard to tell behind the Tinman's mask.

Sarah was on stage all the time now as she was in every scene. When she wasn't rehearsing, she would quickly leave the theater. Jessie never knew where she was going.

* * *

One evening as the Aldens were leaving the auditorium, they noticed a middle-aged woman in a fur coat standing by the stage door.

"Are you looking for someone?" Jessie asked the woman politely.

"Uh, no, not really," the woman answered. "I just came to observe your theater and perhaps see one of your rehearsals," the woman answered.

"Our dress rehearsal is the day after tomorrow," Jessie told her.

"Thank you," the woman replied. "I'll be back then."

As the Aldens walked away, they noticed the woman still standing by the stage door.

"It looks like she knows the Tinman," Henry said as he looked over his shoulder. Jessie and Violet turned around. Down the street by the stage door, they could see the woman talking very intently to Harold, or the Tinman, as everyone now called him. The woman's hand rested lightly on his arm.

"I wonder why she didn't just tell us she

was looking for the Tinman — I mean Harold," Jessie sounded puzzled.

"I was just thinking the same thing," Henry said. He put on his wool mittens and clapped his hands together to keep warm.

Before anyone knew it, the day of the dress rehearsal had arrived. "It's the first rehearsal where we all get to wear our costumes," Jessie said excitedly to Soo Lee.

"Is it always the night before the show?" Soo Lee asked.

"Yes, I think so," Jessie answered as she twirled in front of her bedroom mirror in the lion costume.

"Jessie." Violet took the pins out of her mouth and shook her head laughingly. "If you don't hold still, I can't finish pinning your tail on."

"Oh, sorry." Jessie obediently stopped dancing.

"There." Violet stood back from the costume to observe her handiwork. "I'll sew the tail on when you take off your costume."

"I love your lion costume," Soo Lee said

from her seat on Jessie's bed. She leaned against one of Jessie's lacy white pillows.

"I do, too," Jessie said, touching her furry mane with one paw. "I'm glad to have this part. It's been more fun for me than Dorothy's would have been."

"Grrr, Grrr, Grrrroowl," Benny teased as he came into the room with Henry.

"Looks like you're all ready to go on stage," Henry said.

"I just hope everything goes well tonight," Violet said a little anxiously.

"Well, nothing bad has happened since we found the ruined set," Benny pointed out.

"No," Jessie agreed. "But everyone's been very worried."

Jessie took one more look at her costume in the mirror before she changed back into her regular clothes.

That afternoon, the Aldens, Soo Lee, and Mrs. McGregor arrived early for the dress rehearsal. Most of the cast arrived in plenty of time for Violet and Mrs. Adams to make last-minute adjustments to their costumes.

"Where's Sarah?" Violet asked Jessie as she helped her sister pull back her hair.

"I haven't seen her at all," Jessie said as she pulled on her lion's mask.

Melody stood next to Jessie in the large dressing room. She combed back her thick hair and made a face as she put on the Scarecrow's black felt hat.

"I hate my costume," she said.

"I thought you were getting to like being the Scarecrow," Jessie answered as she smoothed her lion's mane.

"It's not so bad," Melody admitted. "I just wish I could wear a pretty dress."

Nancy poked her head into the dressing room. "Be ready to take your places in the wings, girls," she said. "We're starting in five minutes."

"We're coming," Jessie said.

"Now where on earth is Sarah?" Nancy asked.

"We don't know," Melody answered as she adjusted her hat.

"She hasn't been in the dressing room at all," Violet said.

Mrs. Adams came in wearing her long ivory gown. "Oh, you look beautiful," Jessie and Violet said at once.

"You know, I'm worried about Sarah. She's the only performer who hasn't changed yet. Her costume is still hanging in the costume room," Mrs. Adams said.

Half an hour later, Sarah was still missing.

"I've tried to call her at home, and there's no answer," Jim said, pacing up and down the backstage area. "We'll have to start without her. Melody, you read Sarah's lines in the first scene."

"Should I change into her costume?" Melody asked hopefully.

"No!" Jim almost shouted. "Now, please, get on stage."

At that moment, Sarah rushed through the backstage door. Her eyes were red, and she looked like she'd been crying. The cast and crew stared at her in silence. No one dared say a word.

"Take your place on stage immediately," Jim said quietly to Sarah. "We'll discuss your tardiness later."

Jim turned to the crew. "All right, get ready to raise the curtain."

Henry took his place by the lighting board. During the tornado scene, he dimmed the lights so the stage went black. Then he lit the scenery to make it seem as if dark clouds were moving across the landscape.

Backstage, several crew members, including Benny, rattled a big sheet of aluminum to create the sound of wind. "Tonight, I'm shaking it harder than usual," Benny whispered to Soo Lee. "There's so much wind in a tornado."

Other crew members positioned themselves behind the farmhouse on stage. When Nancy gave the cue, they slowly shook Dorothy's house while the cast screamed and went running for cover.

"I love this scene," Soo Lee whispered to Benny. "It's so exciting."

Benny nodded and rattled the aluminum sheet even harder. "Not so hard there," a crew member said smiling. "It's a tornado, not an earthquake." Benny obediently shook the sheet a little less enthusiastically.

By now the cast was backstage. "Whew, that scene is hard work," Mrs. McGregor confided to Benny and Soo Lee. But she smiled as she said so. The children could tell she was really enjoying her part as Aunt Em.

Sarah and the actors playing the three farmhands were the last to leave the stage. They circled it once more, stomping their feet as they headed into the wings. Henry began to dim the lights to show the scene had ended.

When everyone was off the stage, suddenly, out of nowhere, a large standing spotlight toppled onto the stage, smashing the bulb.

CHAPTER 9

The Show Must Go On

Melody shrieked. Sarah, who was in the wings when the light crashed, turned pale.

Jim jumped onto the stage. "How did this happen?" he demanded, turning to Henry and Stuart.

Both boys gave him a blank look.

Nancy came out of the wings onto the stage. "Do you think someone pushed it over?"

Jim put his hands in front of his face. "I just can't believe someone would do that.

What is going on here!" he yelled. By now, some of the cast and crew had come onto the stage.

Richard stepped to the front of the stage and folded his hands across his chest. "*What is going on here? I could have been killed!*"

"Believe me, Richard, I did not arrange this on purpose," Jim said dryly. "Where are we going to get another spotlight in time for the show tomorrow night?" he added with a sigh.

"Oh, I hadn't even thought of that." Nancy sounded discouraged. She stepped out of the way so the crew members could clear the stage of broken glass.

Once the stage was swept clean, the cast resumed their rehearsal. No one showed much enthusiasm. Many people missed their cues, and even Sarah flubbed her lines in more than one scene.

"Sarah, you weren't supposed to say that!" Melody said loudly.

Henry checked all the overhead lights. "The other lights seem fine," he reported to

Jim after rehearsal. Jim nodded as if he were
still in a daze. Indeed, he looked so tired,
Henry volunteered to stay late to reset the
lighting board.

"We'll help you, Henry," Jessie said. Violet, Benny, and Soo Lee nodded.

"Maybe we'll be able to find another light,"
Violet suggested.

"I wouldn't count on it." Jim sounded discouraged. "I think we better just redesign the
lighting as Henry and I discussed. I know
you'll do a good job — all of you," Jim added
with a grateful look at the Aldens.

When everyone had left, Jessie opened the
door to bring some air into the backstage
area. She poked her head outside. Something
she saw made her quickly shut the door.

"What's the matter?" Violet asked.

"That woman," Jessie whispered. Violet
looked puzzled.

"Remember the woman we saw the other
night in the fur coat?"

Violet nodded. "You mean she's outside
the theater again?"

"Yes," Jessie was still whispering. "She's just waiting in the street."

"Did she see you?" Violet wondered.

Jessie shrugged her shoulders. "I'm not sure."

Violet shivered a little. "It's spooky back here at night," she observed. The girls looked at the large sets stacked along the wall — Dorothy's simple farmhouse, the witch's castle, even the Yellow Brick Road glowed eerily under the light of one small bulb overhead.

Henry came backstage with Benny. "I'm starting to change the lighting so it won't depend so much on that big light we lost."

"Couldn't you wait a little longer?" Jessie asked. "We might find a replacement."

Henry looked at his watch. "Well, all right, but it's already nine o'clock."

Jessie nodded. "I know." Quickly she told her brothers about seeing the mysterious woman in the fur coat.

Henry shook his head. "I don't know what

to think. So many things don't seem right about this play."

"I know what you mean," Jessie answered. She walked over to another storage closet. "Nothing but brooms and mops in here," she announced.

Henry sat down on the steps. "I really think someone tampered with that light on purpose," he said grimly.

"So do I." Jessie's voice sounded muffled from inside the closet. "But who would do such a thing?"

"Why would someone in the cast try to ruin the show for everyone?" Violet remarked.

"We have to think about this," Henry said. "First of all, whoever is doing these things may not be in the cast at all. Who do we suspect besides Sarah and Melody?

"Richard." Violet and Jessie both answered at once. They came to join Henry on the steps.

"We did catch him fiddling with Violet's poster," Jessie reminded them.

"Well, we didn't exactly catch him," Violet pointed out. "But who else would want to make Richard's name bigger?"

Jessie and Henry both nodded.

"What about the Tinman?" Benny asked as he came out of the costume room. "Don't you think it's strange he never takes his costume off?"

"Well, yes," Jessie agreed reluctantly. "Still, I can't believe he'd be responsible for ruining costumes and sets. He's so serious about his acting."

"You could say the same about Sarah," Henry reminded them.

"Yes." Jessie said slowly. "I've been wondering about Sarah ever since the play started. She's so secretive."

"Don't forget about that folder she didn't want us to see," Benny reminded his sister as he joined his family.

"Yes," Jessie nodded.

"But all these pranks were directed *against* Sarah," Violet pointed out. "It's Sarah's costume someone ruined, Sarah's name that was crossed off the audition sheet . . .

"And Sarah's props and script that were taken," Jessie finished.

Henry stood and stretched. "The question is, why wouldn't someone want Sarah in the show?" he asked.

"Well, Melody wouldn't want her," Benny noted.

"No," Jessie agreed. "She wouldn't."

"And Richard wouldn't want her in the play, either, because she takes too much attention away from him," Violet pointed out.

"That's true," Henry said, nodding.

"I guess if we're naming suspects, we can't forget the woman outside in the fur coat," said Violet.

"Or the man in the big white car," Benny remarked.

"Yes," Henry agreed. "I wonder why he didn't want to go backstage to find Sarah himself. No one else would have taken his parking place. No other cars were even parked near his."

"I hadn't thought of that," Violet said slowly. She suddenly stood up and looked around the large backstage area. "By the way, where is Soo Lee?"

"I don't know," Benny said. "Soo Lee! Soo Lee, where are you?" he called loudly.

"I'm in here," answered Soo Lee from the costume room. "I think I found something."

The Aldens rushed to her side. "There's a big trunk in this closet," Soo Lee told them. "Look what's inside!"

"Soo Lee! You found a spare bulb," Henry almost shouted. "I won't have to reset the lights." Henry gave his cousin a big hug. "All we have to do now is replace this light and we're set for tomorrow."

"The show will go on," said Benny happily.

On the night of the performance, Jessie, Mrs. McGregor, and Benny arrived early. They needed plenty of time to change and put on their stage makeup.

Soo Lee came into the auditorium with Henry and Violet. She was all dressed up to be an usher in a red velvet dress and black patent leather shoes.

"I can't thank you enough for finding that light, Soo Lee," Jim said when he saw her.

Soo Lee smiled.

"Goodness, some people are here already," Violet said softly, looking toward the door.

"Oh, I better go seat them," Soo Lee said as she took a stack of programs in her arms.

"We'll be backstage," Henry called to Soo Lee.

From his post by the lighting board, Henry could peek behind the thick red curtain and watch the audience. He was the first to notice Grandfather seated near the front row.

Benny soon came to join Henry. Benny was all dressed up in his Munchkin outfit — pale blue pants and a matching jacket.

"Look, you can see Grandfather," Henry said as he stood near the curtain. Benny peeked out into the auditorium. He looked back at Henry in surprise. "The woman in the fur coat is sitting next to him."

"What?" Henry left his post by the lighting board to look for himself. Sure enough, Grandfather was helping the woman off with her coat. "They're talking like they know each other," Henry said, surprised. "I wonder who that woman could be?"

While Henry stood behind the curtain talking to Benny, he heard some rustling noises behind him. A man wearing a tweed coat was opening the fuse box near the lighting board. He couldn't see Henry or Benny as they were hidden from him by the curtain.

"Hey!" Henry shouted to the man. "What are you doing?"

The man whirled around holding one of the fuses. Henry recognized him. He was the man he'd seen in the big white car. Suddenly, Sarah appeared in the wings with Jessie, Violet, and Jim. She was all dressed in her costume. "Oh, Dad!" she sounded heartbroken. "It was you all along, wasn't it?"

Sarah's father stared at the fuse in his hand and then at the shocked faces of Sarah, Henry, Benny, Jessie, Violet, and Jim.

"Yes," he muttered looking down at the floor. "I couldn't let you be in this play," he continued in a shaky voice. "I just couldn't."

"Why not?" Benny blurted out.

When the man looked up, he had tears in his eyes. "Sarah's my only child," he explained looking at his daughter. "Her mother was an actress. She died in the theater in a freak accident when Sarah was only a baby."

"I knew that, but I still wanted to act!" Sarah exclaimed. She had tears in her eyes, too.

"Ten minutes to curtain time," Nancy called to Henry from behind the backstage curtain. "I'll be ready," Henry called back.

"You almost ruined our production so your daughter couldn't be in the theater!" Jim exclaimed. He couldn't believe it.

Mr. Bellamy sighed. "Yes, I was very upset when I heard Sarah was even trying out for a part. I made that phone call during the auditions and wrote those notes. I used to go backstage after everyone had left for the evening. I stole Sarah's script and tore Dorothy's costume, too."

"How did you get in?"

"I would usually be somewhere in the building before the janitors locked the auditorium."

Jim nodded grimly. "Someone could have been badly hurt when that light toppled over," he said, scowling.

"I know." Mr. Bellamy looked ashamed. "I was so upset, I couldn't think clearly. I can't tell you how sorry I am for all the problems I caused you."

Jim nodded. "Well, I must confess, I am relieved to know the reason for all these disturbances," he said slowly. "At first, I thought this play was jinxed, and no one would ever hire me as a director again."

"Oh, that's why you always looked so worried, even at the very beginning, before the auditions began," Violet said.

Jim smiled and looked a little embarrassed.

Sarah blinked her eyes furiously to keep the tears from running down her cheeks. She went over to her father and put an arm around him. "I really love being with you Dad, but I love acting, too. Please stay for the show. Just watch me. I love the theater so much," Sarah said.

Mr. Bellamy looked at his daughter. "I know you do. I must say I've been impressed with your determination to go on despite all I did to stop you."

"Five minutes to curtain time," Nancy called from behind the curtain.

Mr. Bellamy sighed. "Will you let me stay?" he asked Jim. "I wouldn't blame you for saying no."

"You can stay," Jim said gruffly. He motioned to one of the ushers to lead Mr. Bellamy to a good seat.

"Time to raise the curtain," Jim announced.

"Let's break our legs," Benny said as he took his place in the wings beside the other Munchkins.

CHAPTER 10

Curtain Call

"It's going so much better than the dress rehearsal," Jessie said to Henry as she raced by him between scenes.

"I can tell," Henry said as he brought one of the switches down to the off position.

Nancy caught Jessie's eye and put her finger to her lips. Although she tried to look stern, she couldn't resist giving the Aldens a big smile. Jim had told her about catching Mr. Bellamy before the show, but she had had no time to thank the Aldens. Now she stood in the wings and quickly turned the pages of her script. As stage manager, she had to make sure everyone was on stage at the right time.

When the curtain fell on the final scene, the audience clapped and cheered. Sarah and Harold each received a standing ovation. Indeed, the audience applauded so hard, Sarah and Harold came on stage three times to take their bows. The third time, Sarah received a huge bouquet of red and white roses.

Sarah, Jessie, and Melody hugged one another in the dressing room. Soon the stage doors opened. Friends and relatives streamed backstage to congratulate the performers.

Grandfather stopped into the dressing room with Joe, Alice, Mr. Bellamy, and the woman in the big coat.

"You girls were wonderful," Grandfather told Jessie, Sarah, and Melody. They all beamed at him.

"Sarah, I'm so proud of you," Mr. Bellamy said. He choked a little over his next words. "I was wrong to try to stop you. You're really gifted, just like your mother."

"Oh, Dad, I'm so happy!" Sarah threw her arms around her father and hugged him for a very long time.

"You're going to be even happier." Sarah's father smiled at her as he stepped back to put his hand behind the woman in the big coat. "I'd like to introduce you to Marilyn Morris. She's a theatrical agent from New York. She'd like you to be her client."

"I wrote to you," Sarah said as she shook her agent's hand. She looked dumbfounded. "I sent you my résumé and a picture."

"So *that's* what you had in that mysterious manila folder you wouldn't let us see," Jessie teased. Sarah nodded sheepishly.

"I wrote to Ms. Morris also," Harold said as he came by to offer his congratulations. "I told her she needed to come and discover you." As he finished speaking, Harold lifted off his helmet.

"You're Andrew Tompkins, the Broadway actor! Harold's not your name at all." Sarah could not contain her excitement. "What are you doing here?"

"You're the man we saw in the pizzeria!"

Benny blurted out. "Everyone recognized you except me."

"I had to take a vacation from Broadway for health reasons, but I wanted to do some acting," Andrew explained. "I wanted to go somewhere I wouldn't be recognized. Only Jim knew my secret, but some of you came close to guessing," he added, smiling at the Aldens.

"I think we should all go out to celebrate," Grandfather suggested.

"I agree," Benny said.

"I'll never forget this evening as long as I live," Sarah said, looking pleased and proud.

"None of us will," Jessie said.

"Let's eat," Benny added, smiling happily.

GERTRUDE CHANDLER WARNER discovered when she was teaching that many readers who like an exciting story could find no books that were both easy and fun to read. She decided to try to meet this need, and her first book, *The Boxcar Children*, quickly proved she had succeeded.

Miss Warner drew on her own experiences to write the mystery. As a child she spent hours watching trains go by on the tracks opposite her family home. She often dreamed about what it would be like to set up housekeeping in a caboose or freight car — the situation the Alden children find themselves in.

When Miss Warner received requests for more adventures involving Henry, Jessie, Violet, and Benny Alden, she began additional stories. In each, she chose a special setting and introduced unusual or eccentric characters who liked the unpredictable.

While the mystery element is central to each of Miss Warner's books, she never thought of them as strictly juvenile mysteries. She liked to stress the Aldens' independence and resourcefulness and their solid New England devotion to using up and making do. The Aldens go about most of their adventures with as little adult supervision as possible — something else that delights young readers.

Miss Warner lived in Putnam, Connecticut, until her death in 1979. During her lifetime, she received hundreds of letters from boys and girls telling her how much they liked her books.